Nancy Drew
CLUE BOOK

#1

Pool Party Puzzler

BY CAROLYN KEENE * ILLUSTRATED BY PETER FRANCIS

Aladdin
NEW YORK   LONDON   TORONTO   SYDNEY   NEW DELHI

ALADDIN

An imprint of Simon & Schuster Children's Publishing Division
1230 Avenue of the Americas, New York, NY 10020
This Aladdin paperback edition July 2015
Text copyright © 2015 by Simon & Schuster, Inc.
Illustrations copyright © 2015 by Peter Francis
Also available in an Aladdin hardcover edition.
All rights reserved, including the right of reproduction in whole or in part in any form.
ALADDIN is a trademark of Simon & Schuster, Inc., and related logo is a
registered trademark of Simon & Schuster, Inc.
NANCY DREW, NANCY DREW CLUE BOOK, and colophons are registered trademarks of
Simon & Schuster, Inc.
For information about special discounts for bulk purchases, please contact
Simon & Schuster Special Sales at 1-866-506-1949 or business@simonandschuster.com.
The Simon & Schuster Speakers Bureau can bring authors to your live event. For more information
or to book an event contact the Simon & Schuster Speakers Bureau
at 1-866-248-3049 or visit our website at www.simonspeakers.com.
Book designed by Karina Granda
The text of this book was set in Adobe Garamond Pro.
Manufactured in the United States of America 0615 OFF
2 4 6 8 10 9 7 5 3 1
Library of Congress Control Number 2014026573
ISBN 978-1-4814-3896-4 (hc)
ISBN 978-1-4814-2937-5 (pbk)
ISBN 978-1-4814-2938-2 (eBook)

✳ CONTENTS ✳

Chapter 1

THRONE . . . AND GROANS

"I've heard of sweet sixteen parties before," George Fayne said, "but whoever heard of a sweet *half*-sixteen?"

Nancy Drew looked up from the goody bag she was filling for Deirdre Shannon's sweet half-sixteen party.

"Eight is half of sixteen," Nancy explained. "So since Deirdre is turning eight, she asked her parents for a sweet half-sixteen party!"

"And whatever Deirdre wants," Bess Marvin

said, dropping a fancy iced cookie into a bag, "Deirdre gets!"

It was summer vacation and the theme of Deirdre's party was Beach Party Blast. Nancy, Bess, and George had come extra early to help George's mom cater the party. Louise Fayne had catered lots of kids' birthday parties, but nothing as fancy as this!

"We're eight years old and half-sixteen, too," Nancy pointed out. "And we have something just as awesome as a party like this."

"What?" Bess asked.

"Our own detective club called the Clue Crew!" Nancy answered with a smile.

Nancy, Bess, and George high-fived. The three best friends loved solving mysteries more than anything. They even had their own detective headquarters in Nancy's room!

"And my dad just gave me this brand-new notebook," Nancy said, pulling a notebook with a shiny red cover from her bag. "He told me it would be a good place to write down suspects and

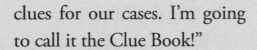

clues for our cases. I'm going to call it the Clue Book!"

Nancy's father wasn't a detective, but he was a lawyer. To Nancy that was the next best thing.

"But we already write down all of our suspects on your computer, Nancy," George pointed out. George loved electronic gadgets more than anything!

"That's true." Nancy nodded. "But we can take the Clue Book with us wherever we go. It will make us even *better* detectives!"

"Okay, if we're such great detectives," George said, "then why are we all dressed up so goofy?"

"Deirdre asked everyone to wear sea costumes over our swimsuits," Nancy reminded her. "I'm a sea horse, Bess is a sea fairy, and you're a—"

"Jellyfish!" George groaned. The ribbon tentacles streaming from her hat wiggled over her face. "Don't remind me."

Nancy brushed aside her reddish-blond bangs to look around for Deirdre. She was probably getting ready for her grand entrance. Mrs. Fayne said it would be at one o'clock sharp—after the guests arrived.

"Great job, girls," Mrs. Fayne said after all the goody bags had been stuffed and placed on a table. "Why don't you explore the yard before the others get here?"

Nancy smiled as she looked around the Shannons' backyard. It looked more like a beach than a yard. There was real white sand and beach umbrellas around the pool. On each party table was a sand castle centerpiece surrounded by shells and starfish. Inflated palm trees dotted the lawn. So did some of Deirdre's birthday presents—like a shiny lavender electric scooter with a matching helmet!

"This party is going to be amazing," George said. "I'll bet every kid in River Heights is invited."

"Every kid but Shelby Metcalf," Nancy said. "Deirdre is still mad at Shelby for not trading lunches with her at school one day."

"What kind of lunches?" Bess asked.

"Shelby had peanut butter and jelly," Nancy explained. "Deirdre had a soggy spinach salad."

George suddenly stopped walking. "Hey, check it out!" she said, pointing to something in the distance.

Nancy and Bess looked to see where George was pointing. A woman wearing a sun hat was busily snipping hedges behind the pool. The three hedges were shaped like sea creatures!

"Let's get a closer look!" Nancy said excitedly.

The girls hurried over to the woman. She was in the middle of trimming the claw on a hedge shaped like a crab.

"Hello," Bess said. "Are you a gardener?"

"I'm what they call a garden designer," the woman replied with a cheery smile. "My name is Taffy, and I create topiaries." She pointed at one of the leafy hedges.

"To-pi-ar-ies," Nancy repeated.

"Topiaries by Taffy," Taffy said proudly. "That's the name of my company!"

"Did Deirdre see these topiaries yet?" George asked.

"If she did," Bess said, "I'd bet she loved them!"

But Taffy shook her head and heaved a sigh.

"Deirdre wasn't very happy with my topiaries," Taffy said. "She wanted one of them to look like her!"

"You mean she wanted a grassy statue of herself?" George asked.

Taffy nodded and said, "Deirdre said she was Queen of the Sea and her party had to be *perfect*."

"That sounds like Deirdre, all right," Bess said.

"Oh well," Taffy said. She gave her topiary

one final snip. "I guess I'll have to surprise Queen Deirdre later."

Nancy wondered what the surprise would be. Before she got a chance to ask, Bess shook Nancy's arm.

"The other guests are here!" Bess announced.

Nancy turned to see other kids dressed like sea creatures in the Shannons' backyard. The most awesome party of the year was about to begin!

After saying a quick good-bye to Taffy, the girls ran to join the others. Many were dancing. Some were sipping smoothies.

Nancy recognized Kendra Jackson, Marcy Rubin, and Henderson Murphy from school. But there was one kid no one knew.

"Who's that?" George asked. She nodded toward a kid wearing a green sea monster costume. A mask and headdress totally covered his or her face. Both hands were stuffed inside gloves with long webbed fingers!

"I know how we can find out," Nancy said

with a smile. "Let's go over and say hi."

The girls walked over to the sea monster kid.

"Hi, there. That's a neat costume," Bess said kindly. "But aren't you hot in it?"

The kid shook his or her head, then walked away without a word.

"We still don't know who she is," Bess said.

"How do you know she's a *she*?" Nancy asked.

"Her feet weren't covered," Bess said. "Did you see her purple sandals and pink toenail polish? Totally girlie-girl."

"Like you, Bess!" George teased. "Only *you* would notice purple sandals and pink toenail polish!"

Nancy giggled. Bess and George were cousins but totally different. Bess had blond hair and blue eyes, and she loved clothes more than anything. George had dark eyes and curly hair. She was fine with new clothes as long as they had enough pockets for her electronic gadgets!

"I have an idea," Nancy suggested. "Let's get some smoothies—before the tropical ones are gone."

"Last one there is a rotten coconut!" George declared.

They were about to run to the party's special smoothie stand when a big voice boomed through a DJ's speakers. "Attention, kids! Let's give it up for everybody's favorite sweet half-sixteen birthday girl, Queen Deirdre of the Sea!"

"It's Deirdre's grand entrance!" Nancy said excitedly. She glanced at her watch. It was one o'clock. "And right on schedule!"

The kids gathered on the patio to watch. A trumpet blared as four teenagers wearing huge fish headdresses marched around the side of the house. In each of their hands was a pole. Resting atop the four poles was a giant half-shell throne!

Nancy couldn't believe her eyes. Waving down from the elaborate shell was Deirdre. The birthday girl was dressed in a glitzy mermaid costume and shell-covered crown!

"Awesome!" Nancy exclaimed.

The teens made a sudden sharp turn and the

throne tipped. Deirdre screamed as it swayed back and forth!

"Oh, noooo!" Nancy shrieked as she covered her eyes. "Queen Deirdre is going to fall!"

Chapter

2

NOT COOL IN THE POOL

"Steady, you guys!" one of the teens shouted. "Bring it down easy . . . nice and easy."

Nancy peeked out from between her fingers. Both the shell throne and Deirdre were slowly being lowered onto the ground.

The party guests sighed with relief. But Deirdre hopped off the throne hopping mad!

"You should have been more careful. After all, you were carrying a queen's throne!" Deirdre scolded. "Not some tray at Crabby Carl's!"

Deirdre gave the teens one last glare and ran off to join her friends. The four teens stood to the side, frowns on their faces.

"I thought those fish hats looked familiar," Bess said. "Those teenagers are waiters at Crabby Carl's Seafood Restaurant!"

"The waiters look pretty crabby right now," George whispered. "After being yelled at by Queen Deirdre."

"I feel bad for the fish teens," Nancy said. "Let's tell them they did a great job!"

Nancy, Bess, and George walked toward the teenagers. As they got nearer they heard them talking in lowered voices.

"Deirdre Shannon has been bossing us around since we started practicing," a girl was saying.

"She's a queen, all right," another girl said. "The queen of mean!"

"Forget about it," one boy said. He flashed a sly smile. "Because it's time to carry out our secret plan."

The teens' fish headdresses wiggled as they

bumped fists. They then turned and walked around to the side of the house.

"Secret plan?" Nancy asked. "What secret plan?"

"It wouldn't be a secret if we knew!" George shrugged.

Nancy wanted to know. She was about to suggest following the teens when—

"Attention, kids!" Mrs. Shannon shouted into a bullhorn. "Please follow Queen Deirdre into the house so you can hang up your costumes."

"Then everybody into the pool!" Deirdre cried, her hands waving in the air.

The kids cheered. Nancy forgot about the teens and their secret plan as she, Bess, and George followed Deirdre and the others.

As they walked around the swimming pool, Nancy glanced into the water. It was crystal clear all the way down to the bottom. Perfect for swimming!

"Hey, you guys," George said, interrupting Nancy's thoughts. "There's the sea monster."

Nancy turned to see the kid in the sea monster costume. Instead of following the others, the monster lagged behind.

"Aren't you coming too?" Nancy called.

The sea monster shook her head, which was still totally covered.

"Oh well," Nancy said as she and her friends continued walking. "Maybe she didn't bring her swimsuit."

"I brought three suits," Bess said with a smile. "The one under my costume plus two other options."

"Give me a break!" George groaned.

Once inside the house, the kids hung up their costumes. Nancy carefully put the Clue Book into her bag, and hung up her bag beside her costume. George couldn't wait to get out of her jellyfish suit!

"Hurry up, hurry up!" Deirdre cried. She was now wearing a bright blue swimsuit with her Queen of the Sea crown. "My parents have *another* big surprise for me outside."

"Bigger than the electric scooter?" Henderson asked.

"I hope so!" Deirdre said. She gave a little jump and squealed, "You guys—is my super sweet half-sixteen party perfect or what?"

When all the costumes were hung on racks, Deirdre rushed everyone to the back door. Deirdre was the first outside for her latest surprise. Nancy could see Deirdre's jaw drop as she stared straight ahead.

Nancy followed Deirdre's gaze. What she saw was a beautiful mermaid seated on a gold throne decorated with pink and silver seashells!

"Happy birthday, Deirdre!" the mermaid called as she waved. "It's so good to 'sea' you. That's s-e-a, as in the ocean. Hee-hee!"

Deirdre turned to her parents. "You got me a mermaid?" she asked.

"Not just *any* mermaid, honey," Mr. Shannon said. "It's Marissa—Queen of the Mermaids!"

"I've come to swim for you all today!" Mermaid Marissa exclaimed, still waving her hand.

"Okay, kids," Mrs. Shannon called to the guests. "Who wants to meet Queen Marissa?"

"Me, me, me!" everyone shouted.

Nancy, Bess, and George raced straight to Queen Marissa's throne with the others. Those with cameras or phones took pictures of the glittering mermaid.

"How about a picture with the birthday girl?" Mr. Shannon asked, holding up a camera. He looked around. "Where did Deirdre disappear to, anyway?"

"Over here!" Deirdre shouted.

Nancy turned to see Deirdre squeezing through the crowd. When she reached the mermaid's throne she flashed a smile for the camera.

"And now," Queen Marissa said with a shake of her fin, "it's time for my spectacular deep-sea swim show!"

The DJ played soft music as bubbles drifted from machines. Excited whispers also filled the air as Queen Marissa hobbled across the diving board. When she reached the edge, she raised both hands gracefully above her head.

"She's going to dive!" Nancy said.

"I've never seen a mermaid swim before," Bess said.

"This is going to be good," George declared.

Marissa gave a little hop. But just as she was about to jump, she froze to a stop.

"Look!" Marissa screamed as she pointed down at the water. "At the bottom of the pool. Th-th-there's a snake!"

Chapter

3

SNAKY SHOCKER

Everyone began talking at once.

"In the pool?"

"A real live snake?"

"No way!"

Mr. and Mrs. Shannon kept the kids away from the pool, but the green and yellow snake coiled at the bottom wasn't hard to see.

"Ew!" Bess shrieked.

"You don't see that every day!" George said.

That's for sure, Nancy thought. She knew she hadn't seen a snake in the pool when she had looked in it earlier!

Mr. Shannon rushed to help Queen Marissa off the diving board. He tried to apologize, but she wouldn't hear it.

"I'm out of here!" Marissa declared. "No more kiddie parties for me—ever!"

Nancy couldn't take her eyes off of the snake. It wasn't moving. And it looked like something was hanging from its tail!

"Mr. and Mrs. Shannon?" Nancy called. "I think that snake has a tag on its tail."

"A tag?" Mr. Shannon said.

Using a skimmer, one of the caterers helped fish the snake out of the pool. The snake did have a tag on its tail—a price tag!

"Guess what, boys and girls?" Mr. Shannon chuckled with relief. "This snake is a fake!"

"It sure is!" Mrs. Shannon said, reading the tag. "It's from Yuks Joke Shop on Main Street!"

"Some joke!" Deirdre snapped. She turned

to glare at her party guests. "Okay, which one of you jokers threw that fake snake into the pool?"

The kids stared blankly at Deirdre, not saying a word. Some mumbled "Not me" or "Nuh-uh."

Mrs. Shannon put a gentle hand on Deirdre's shoulder.

"Deirdre, dear," she said. "Why don't we forget about that silly snake and continue with the pool party?"

"Well . . . ," Deirdre muttered. "Okay."

"You heard the queen!" Mr. Shannon boomed with a smile. "Everybody into the pool!"

Deirdre was smiling again as the kids grabbed swim rafts and floatation noodles. But as the others hopped into the pool, Nancy, Bess, and George stood to the side, talking softly.

"I think Deirdre was right," Nancy admitted. "Someone here must have thrown that snake into the pool."

"Maybe it wasn't just a dumb joke either,"

George said. "Maybe somebody wanted to ruin Deirdre's party."

"Who would want to ruin an awesome party like this one?" Bess asked.

"I don't know," Nancy said. "But I think the Clue Crew should find out."

Bess gave a little hop as she clapped her hands. Parties were fun, but so were solving mysteries— especially for the Clue Crew!

"Okay," George said. "Let's tell Deirdre we're on the case."

"I'm sure she'll be happy we want to help!" Bess said.

But when Nancy, Bess, and George offered to find the snake slinger, Deirdre shook her head.

"This is a pool party!" Deirdre replied firmly. "Not some mystery party!"

Nancy, Bess, and George stared openmouthed at Deirdre as she huffed away. Still wearing her crown, she jumped into the pool with a big splash.

"I guess she doesn't want us to solve this mystery." Bess sighed.

"Deirdre may not want to solve this mystery," Nancy said. "But I do."

"So do I," George said. She cracked a little smile. "If you ask me, something *fishy* is going on around here."

"George, puh-leeze!" Bess groaned.

The girls didn't want to leave the party for their detective headquarters. Instead they discussed the case floating on a lobster raft in the pool.

"I'm sure the snake was thrown in right before Queen Marissa's show," Nancy said.

"Probably while we were all in the house."

"How do you know?" George asked.

"I peeked in the pool right before we went inside," Nancy explained. "The water looked great. There were no snakes!"

The lobster raft drifted past other kids splashing in the pool. Everybody looked so happy—not angry or mean!

"I still don't get it," Bess said. "Who would want to ruin such a great party?"

"Maybe somebody who was mad at Deirdre," Nancy said with a shrug.

"Everybody is mad at Deirdre at some point," George said. "She's always yelling at people."

Yelling? Nancy's eyes lit up at the word.

"What about the waiters from Crabby Carl's?" Nancy suggested. "They were mad at Deirdre for yelling at them."

"And they said something about a secret plan," Bess added. "Maybe their plan was that icky snake."

"The waiters are our first suspects," George

declared. "But who else would want to ruin Deirdre's party?"

"It could have been any of these kids," Bess said, looking out at the swimmers. "But if we were all in the house at the time of the crime—"

"But we weren't all in the house!" Nancy cut in. "Remember the sea monster? She didn't want to come inside!"

"We never saw her again after that either," George pointed out.

"The sea monster is our next suspect," Bess declared. "Whoever she is."

"I want to make a list of our suspects like we always do," George said.

"Let's get the Clue Book!" Nancy said.

"Come on. I left it in the house."

The girls left the lobster raft floating in the pool as they stepped out. On the way they passed by Taffy's topiaries. Nancy's favorite was the angelfish. But just as she went to get a closer look . . .

"Nancy!" Bess cried. "Watch out!"

Chapter

SOMETHING FISHY

"What?" Nancy asked. She looked down and gasped. Curled up in the grass just inches away from her feet was another snake!

"Omigosh! Omigosh!" Bess cried.

"Calm down," George said. "That one is fake too!"

George pointed to the Yuks price tag on the snake's tail. It was also the same color as the snake in the pool—green and yellow!

"There's one more!" Nancy exclaimed, pointing

to another fake snake by the second topiary. The girls checked out the third one but didn't find any fake snake.

"Do you think Taffy planted all these snakes?" Nancy asked. "The one in the pool, too?"

"Why would Taffy want to spoil Deirdre's party?" Bess asked.

"Taffy told us that Deirdre didn't like her topiaries," Nancy said. "Then Taffy said she had a surprise for Deirdre."

"Maybe Taffy's surprise was the fake snake in the pool!" George said. "I guess Taffy is our next suspect."

"Do you still want to write down the list of suspects in the Clue Book, Nancy?" Bess asked.

"I'd rather go back to the party," Nancy admitted. "Even detectives need a break once in a while."

"Especially after finding those snakes!" Bess shuddered.

The rest of the party was awesome. The girls didn't find any more fake snakes. Deirdre seemed happy too as she thanked her guests for coming to her "perfect" super sweet half-sixteen party.

After the party Nancy, Bess, and George helped Mrs. Fayne and the caterers pack up all the leftover food and supplies. They were happy to snack on some extra cookies and mini quiche while Nancy listed all their suspects in the Clue Book. At the top of the list she wrote:

1. Crabby Carl's waiters

Then she wrote:

2. Taffy of Taffy's Topiaries
3. Sea monster

"I'd like to stop off at Crabby Carl's," Mrs. Fayne said as she drove the girls home in her catering van. "Those waiters worked so hard that I think they deserve some cupcakes."

Nancy, Bess, and George traded looks. The waiters at Crabby Carl's were suspects!

"Um, we can drop off the cupcakes, Mrs. Fayne!"

Nancy blurted. "We want to visit Crabby Carl's anyway."

"Why?" Mrs. Fayne asked, sounding surprised.

"Er, to visit Crusty the lobster," George said quickly. "You know, the lobster that's been in their tank for years and years."

"We love Crusty!" Bess added.

"Okay, okay." Mrs. Fayne chuckled. "Crabby Carl's is within five blocks of our house."

"Thanks, Mrs. Fayne!" Nancy exclaimed.

Nancy, Bess, and George had the same rule: They could walk anywhere without an adult as long as it was within five blocks of home and as long as they were together.

"Be careful with those cupcakes," Mrs. Fayne warned as she dropped off the girls at Crabby Carl's. "And say hi to Crusty for me!"

"We will, Mom!" George called as she carried the big box of cupcakes.

Nancy, Bess, and George walked through a pair of swinging doors into the restaurant. Tables were filled with people eating fish, hush puppies, and Nancy's favorite popcorn shrimp!

"Can I help you?" someone with a gruff voice asked.

Nancy, Bess, and George turned to see Crabby Carl, the owner of the restaurant. He got his nickname because he hardly ever smiled, but his food was great!

"What are those? Cupcakes?" Carl asked, staring through the box's cellophane cover. "We serve our own desserts here."

"I know," George said. "My mom is a caterer."

"And she wants the waiters who worked at Deirdre Shannon's party to have these cupcakes," Nancy added.

"Cupcakes for the waiters?" Carl growled. "What about for me? I own the place!"

"If they're nice, they'll share!" Bess said.

"Okay," Carl said. He nodded to the back of the

restaurant and said, "You can bring the cupcakes to the waiters' break room. The ones who worked at the party are busy serving customers now, but they should be taking their break any minute now."

"Thank you, Mr. Crabby," Nancy said.

The girls were about to head to the back when they noticed something strange. For the first time the lobster tank in the restaurant was empty.

"What happened to Crusty?" George asked.

"I don't know." Crabby Carl sighed sadly. "One minute Crusty was in the tank; the next minute he was gone!"

CRUSTY

As the girls headed to the back, Bess whispered, "You don't think someone ate Crusty, do you?"

"Who would want to eat Crusty?" George demanded. "He's like a celebrity here!"

The waiters' break room was next to the kitchen. George opened the door, and the girls stepped inside. They looked around and saw a lumpy brown sofa, table, TV, fridge, and a wooden room divider that looked like a screen.

"The waiters aren't here yet," Nancy said as George placed the cupcake box on the table. "Let's look for clues!"

"What kind of clues?" Bess asked.

"Start searching for fake snakes," George suggested. "Maybe there's a box of them around here somewhere."

Nancy, Bess, and George searched the room until they heard voices outside the door.

"The waiters are coming!" George whispered. "Let's hide so we can listen to what they say."

The three friends darted behind the screen.

They peeked out through the screen's wooden slats. Four waiters were stepping into the room wearing fish headdresses.

"That's them," George hissed. "The same waiters from the party!"

"I hope they don't find us snooping," Bess whispered.

The girls were as quiet as mice as they listened. Nancy couldn't resist taking out the Clue Book. She wanted to make sure to write down anything important that the waiters said.

"Mission accomplished, you guys," a boy said. "And nobody had a clue it was us!"

Nancy shot her friends a sideways glance. Was their mission putting the snake into Deirdre's pool?

"Now it's on to Plan B!" the boy went on.

"Plan B?" Nancy whispered. "What's Plan B?"

The girls peered through the slats again. This time they all gasped. The waiters were walking toward them! One of the waiters carried a big white container, which she placed on the ground just a few inches from Nancy.

Another waiter suddenly stopped. She pointed to the table and said, "Cupcakes! Let's have some before we get started on our plan."

As the waiters helped themselves to the cupcakes, George tugged on Nancy's elbow.

"Look!" George whispered. She nodded toward the white container. "Maybe the fake snakes are in there!"

Nancy, Bess, and George gathered around the container. Cold air blasted out as George pulled off the lid. Inside was a pile of ice and something else. . . .

"Holy cannoli," George whispered.

"It's a giant cockroach!" Bess cried.

"That's not a cockroach!" Nancy said. She stared down at the dark red creature waving its claws. "That's *Crusty*!"

Chapter

TOE *NAILED*

The girls shrieked as Crusty tried crawling out of the container. They ran out from behind the screen one by one.

When the waiters saw the girls, they froze with the cupcakes still in their hands. Nancy could see their names stitched on their aprons: NICOLE, KIERAN, TODD, and JESSICA.

"Um . . . hi." Nancy gulped.

"What are you kids doing here?" Nicole demanded.

"We brought those cupcakes you're eating," George said.

"Yummy, huh?" Bess asked.

"If you just brought cupcakes," Todd said, "why were you hiding?"

"We wanted to find out who threw the fake snake into Deirdre's pool," George said bravely. "Was it you guys?"

"There was a fake snake in Deirdre Shannon's pool?" Todd asked, sounding surprised.

"I'm sorry we missed that!" Nicole chuckled.

"You should be sorry," Bess said. "It almost ruined Deirdre's party."

"I am sorry about that," Nicole admitted. "But it wasn't us."

"We left right after Deirdre's grand entrance," Jessica said. "We didn't see any snakes in the pool."

"But we know Deirdre yelled at you," Nancy said. "We also heard you talking about some secret plan."

The four waiters began to laugh.

"What's so funny?" George demanded.

"Our secret plan is to free Crusty before his sixtieth birthday," Jessica explained.

"Free Crusty?" Nancy repeated.

"Carl doesn't know it," Jessica said in a hushed voice. "But I'm going to take Crusty on our family vacation to the sea tomorrow."

"You mean you're going to throw him back into the ocean?" Bess asked, wide-eyed.

"Sure thing," Kieran replied. "Crusty is going to love it!"

Nancy understood it now. So that's why Crusty wasn't in his tank. He was about to be freed!

Suddenly, Kieran pointed over Nancy's, Bess's, and George's shoulders and cried, "There's Crusty!"

Nancy, Bess, and George whirled around. Crusty the lobster had escaped the container and was scrambling across the floor!

"Crusty can't be out of that container for long!" Kieran exclaimed. "We've got to put him back on ice now!"

But Crusty had other plans. The lobster picked

up speed and took off. Nancy, Bess, and George watched the waiters chase Crusty through the room.

"The waiters seem nice," Nancy whispered. "But how do we know they really left after Deirdre's grand entrance?"

"I know how we can find out," George whispered. "Follow me."

The waiters were still chasing Crusty as the girls walked over to a clock on the wall.

"This is called a time clock," George explained. "The waiters stick a card inside, and it prints the time they got to work."

A rack of time cards hung next to the clock. Quickly and quietly the girls found the cards for Nicole, Kieran, Todd, and Jessica.

"Deirdre's grand entrance was at one o'clock sharp," Nancy whispered. "These cards show that the waiters got to work at one thirty."

"So they *did* go straight to work," Bess whispered.

Suddenly—

"Gotcha!" Jessica shouted as she grabbed Crusty. The waiters cheered until someone else burst into the room. It was Carl . . . and he looked crabby!

"What's that racket back here?" Carl said. His eyes flew wide open when he saw the lobster in Jessica's hands. "Cheese and crackers! Is that Crusty?"

"Um . . . ," Todd started to say.

Nicole stalled. "Well . . ."

"Time to go," Nancy murmured to Bess and George.

The girls left the break room and the restaurant. As they stepped outside, George said, "So the fish are off the hook. What next?"

"It's getting late," Nancy said. "Let's work on the case tomorrow."

"Good idea, Nancy," George said. "I'm getting hungry for dinner—even after all that party food."

"What are you eating tonight, George?" Bess asked.

"Anything but lobster!" George groaned.

"Would you like grilled veggies with your burger, Nancy?" Mr. Drew called from the grill in the backyard. He was wearing the DUDE WITH THE FOOD apron Nancy had given him for Father's Day.

"Yes, thanks, Daddy!" Nancy said. "I'd also like some help with the Clue Crew's new case, please."

"One order of mystery advice coming right up!" Mr. Drew declared.

As Nancy played on the grass with her puppy, Chocolate Chip, she explained the case of the fake snake in the pool. She had already crossed off the waiters' names from the list of suspects in the Clue Book:

1. ~~Crabby Carl's waiters~~
2. Taffy of Taffy's Topiaries
3. Sea monster

"The waiters didn't do it," Nancy said. "We already figured that out."

"Do you have any other suspects?" Mr. Drew asked.

"We have two more, Daddy," Nancy replied. "One is Taffy the garden designer. The other is that mysterious kid in the sea monster costume."

Hannah Gruen smiled as she carried a bowl of fruit salad into the backyard. Hannah was much more than the Drew's housekeeper; she was almost like a mother to Nancy. That's because Nancy's real mother died when she was only three years old.

"Do you know the sea monster kid's name?" Hannah asked.

Nancy shook her head and said, "All we know is that she likes pink toenail polish, Hannah. That's not much."

Chip's ears suddenly perked up. She wagged her tail, then raced away and around the side of the house.

"Chip, come back!" Nancy called. "You're not on a leash!"

Nancy chased Chip to the front yard. Chip was still wagging her tail and barking toward the sidewalk. Walking past the Drew's house was Shelby Metcalf.

"Hi, Shelby," Nancy said, holding on to Chip's collar. Her puppy seemed to know all of Nancy's friends!

"Oh, uh, hi, Nancy," Shelby said. She didn't look like she wanted to talk but stopped anyway. "Um . . . how was Deirdre's party?"

Nancy had totally forgotten that Shelby hadn't been invited to Deirdre's party. What could she say that wouldn't make Shelby feel bad?

"Um . . . it was okay," Nancy said with a shrug.

But as Nancy lowered her eyes she saw something that made her gasp. Shelby was wearing purple sandals. And her toenails were painted pink!

Omigosh, Nancy thought, her heart pounding. *Just like the sea monster!*

Chapter 6

LITTLE RIDDLE

Nancy looked back up at Shelby's face.

Could she have been the kid in the sea monster costume? Was she at Deirdre's party after all?

"Shelby, what did you do today?" Nancy blurted.

"Nothing," Shelby blurted back. She started walking. "I've got to go now."

Nancy's head was spinning with questions as she watched Shelby walk up the block and turn the corner.

Could Shelby have been mad at Deirdre because she wasn't invited to Deirdre's sweet half-sixteen party? Did Shelby secretly crash Deirdre's party so she could throw the snake into Deirdre's pool?

"I don't want Shelby to be a suspect, Chip." Nancy sighed. "But it looks like she already is!"

"Woof!" Chip barked.

"Are you sure it was the same *pink* toenail polish the sea monster wore, Nancy?" Bess asked the next day as the Clue Crew headed to

Main Street. "There's cotton candy pink, hot pink, ballet pink—"

"It was pink, Bess!" Nancy cut in. "That's all I know."

"I just hope we find Shelby so we can ask her a few questions," George said.

"We will," Nancy assured her. "Shelby's mom told us she had an errand to run on Main Street."

It was Monday morning. It was also summer vacation, so the girls didn't have school. Instead they had all day to work on their case. The Clue Book was safely tucked inside Nancy's bag as she walked along. She had already added Shelby's name to the list of suspects:

1. ~~Crabby Carl's waiters~~
2. Taffy of Taffy's Topiaries
3. Sea monster
4. Shelby Metcalf

"Why would Shelby go to Deirdre's party if she wasn't invited?" Bess wondered.

"Maybe Shelby was mad at Deirdre for not inviting her," Nancy figured. "Mad enough to do something not-so-nice."

"You guys, look!" George said as they reached Main Street. She pointed at Yuks Joke Shop. Coiled in the store window was a green and yellow fake snake.

"That snake looks just like the ones at the party!" Nancy said. "Let's ask the owner if anyone bought a bunch of them lately."

A bell over the door jingled as Nancy, Bess, and George walked inside. Sitting behind a counter was a woman wearing a pirate bandana and an eye patch. On her Yuks T-shirt was a badge that read DEBBIE.

"Ahoy, me kiddies!" Debbie greeted in a pirate-like voice. "What brings you landlubbers to drop anchor at Yuks?"

"Snakes," Bess said.

"We would like to know who bought a bunch of fake snakes," Nancy explained. "Maybe you can tell us his or her name?"

"And not in pirate talk, please," George added. "This is serious business."

Debbie stared at the girls with her uncovered eye. She then shook her head.

"I can't give you that person's name," Debbie said. "But since this is a joke store I *can* give you a riddle."

"A riddle?" Nancy repeated.

"What's sweet, sticky, and really stretchy?" Debbie asked with a smile.

"Sweet?" Bess repeated.

"Sticky?" Nancy asked.

"Really stretchy?" George said.

The girls pondered the riddle. Then—

"Taffy!" the girls said at the same time.

They were about to high-five when the bell jingled again. Turning toward the door, they saw Shelby!

Shelby stared at Nancy, Bess, and George. Hanging from her hand was a Yuks shopping bag.

"Uh . . . I think I'm in the wrong store!" Shelby said, backing out of the door.

The girls thanked Debbie before following Shelby outside.

"Do you buy a lot of things at Yuks, Shelby?" Nancy asked her.

"What's in the bag, Shelby?" George asked.

"Library books," Shelby mumbled. "I have to return them so they're not overdue."

"When will they be overdue?" Bess asked.

"In five minutes!" Shelby said.

As Shelby dashed off, Nancy looked at the shopping bag in Shelby's hand. It didn't seem to be filled with books. Books would have made the bag look heavier than it did.

"Shelby will never tell us whether or not she was at Deirdre's party yesterday," Bess said.

"Oh yeah?" George said. "Watch this!"

The girls hurried to catch up with Shelby.

"Too bad you weren't at Deirdre's party, Shelby,"

George said. "Her parents surprised her with a real live dolphin named Marissa!"

"Dolphin?" Shelby said. She stopped walking. "You mean it was a *mermaid* named Mar—"

Shelby stopped mid-sentence. She clapped a hand over her mouth and mumbled, "Me and my big mouth."

"It's okay, Shelby," Nancy said gently. "How did you know it was a mermaid? Were you at Deirdre's party?"

Shelby didn't answer. Instead she began to run!

"Shelby!" Nancy shouted after her. "Please— wait up!"

Chapter

7

SHELBY'S SECRET

Shelby was a superfast runner. Nancy, Bess, and George ran fast too, but they couldn't catch up.

"Shelby, we just want to ask you something!" Nancy called as they ran.

"I have nothing to say!" Shelby cried as she reached the end of the block. Just then a dog walker with six dogs came around the corner. Two dogs jumped up on Shelby, knocking the bag out of her hand.

"Oh no!" Shelby groaned as a glove and some other items fell out onto the sidewalk.

"I'm so sorry!" the dog walker said, tugging the pooches away from Shelby. As the dog walker and the dogs walked away, the Clue Crew raced over.

George pointed to the glove as well as other pieces of clothing scattered on the ground. "Hey!" she said. "That's the same sea monster costume we saw at the party yesterday."

"So?" Shelby said.

"So were you at Deirdre's party yesterday, Shelby?" Nancy asked nicely.

"We may be detectives, Shelby," Bess said with a little smile. "But we're still your friends. You can tell us."

Shelby cast her eyes downward and nodded.

"I *was* there," Shelby admitted. "Just now I was trying to return the costume I borrowed from Yuks. The one I wore to Deirdre's party."

"Why did you come if you weren't invited?" Bess asked.

"Because I didn't want to miss the best party ever!" Shelby wailed. "So I disguised myself and snuck in."

Nancy suddenly knew why Shelby wouldn't come into Deirdre's house. If Shelby had hung up her costume, everybody would have known it was her.

"What did you do while we all went into the house?" Nancy asked.

"I just hung around outside," Shelby said. "But I left after Queen Marissa showed up. My costume was crazy hot. I couldn't play games or talk to anyone, so I wasn't having fun."

"Did you really just hang around?" George asked. "Or did you throw that snake into Deirdre's pool?"

"Snake?" Shelby gasped. "What snake? Where? Where?"

Nancy was about to explain when Shelby began to shake all over.

"Oh no!" Shelby cried. "I hate snakes more than anything in the whole wide world!"

Shelby was still shaking as she began picking up her spilled costume.

"Shelby's really afraid of snakes," Nancy whispered as she, Bess, and George huddled a few feet away.

"She's got to be afraid of snakes to act like that," Bess murmured. "Unless she's just a good actress."

"No way," George whispered. "Remember when Shelby played Tinker Bell in the class play? She forgot almost all her lines!"

Nancy noticed one of the sea monster gloves

near their feet. Picking up the glove, Nancy studied it. The pointy sea monster fingers were webbed together almost like a duck's feet!

"Shelby couldn't have picked up a squirmy fake snake with fingers like these!" Nancy said, holding the sea monster glove. "She couldn't have thrown it into the pool either."

The Clue Crew walked back to Shelby.

"It was just a fake snake, Shelby," Nancy said, handing Shelby back the sea monster glove. "And we know you didn't throw it into Deirdre's pool."

Shelby gave a little smile.

"And guess what?" Bess said. "We're going to invite you to all our birthday parties from now on."

"Really?" Shelby asked.

"Sure!" Bess said. She smiled as she pointed to Shelby's feet. "As long as you let me borrow that awesome pink toenail polish!"

"Deal!" Shelby laughed.

The Clue Crew was happy that Shelby was no longer a suspect.

But as they were about to walk her back to Yuks—

VROOOOOOOM!!!!

Nancy, Bess, George, and Shelby whirled around. Speeding down the sidewalk on her fancy lavender electric scooter was Deirdre Shannon!

"Out of my waaaaaay!" Deirdre shouted from the scooter. "I can't stop this thing!!"

Chapter

A-MAZE-ING!

Nancy, Bess, George, and Shelby jumped to the side.

"Step on the brake!" George shouted to Deirdre as she came zooming down the block. "Step on the brake, Deirdre!"

Deirdre screeched to a stop inches away from the girls. She took a deep breath, then removed her matching lavender helmet as if nothing had happened.

"Hi," Deirdre said. She looked directly at

Shelby. "Too bad you couldn't come to my perfect sweet half-sixteen party, Shelby."

"Yeah, too bad," Shelby said with a frown.

"Oh, but don't worry," Deirdre went on. "You can read all about my perfect sweet half-sixteen party on my famous blog, *Dishing with Deirdre*!"

Nancy rolled her eyes. Who at school *didn't* know the name of Deirdre's blog? She was the only eight-year-old kid in River Heights with one!

"I've got to go now," Shelby said. She gave Nancy, Bess, and George a quick wink. "To return my library books."

"See you, Shelby," Nancy said with a smile.

As Shelby walked away, Deirdre pulled her lavender-colored helmet back onto her head.

"I was just trying out my awesome new birthday present," Deirdre told the girls. "What were you doing?"

"As a matter of fact," George said, "we were looking for the person who threw the fake snake into your pool."

"Do you want to hear what we know so far,

Deirdre?" Nancy asked, pulling the Clue Book from her bag.

Deirdre shook her head. "I told you!" she groaned. "I don't care who did it. I just want to forget about it. My party was perfect, and that's all that counts."

"But Queen Marissa's water show was ruined because of the snake!" Bess said.

"*Queen* Marissa?" Deirdre cried. "There was only *one* queen at my party and that was me: Queen Deirdre of the Sea! So just let it go, okay?"

Deirdre flicked a switch on her scooter and

zoomed off. Nancy watched her zigzag down the block, and sighed.

"I don't get it," Nancy said. "Doesn't Deirdre want to know who tried to ruin her party?"

"Forget it, Nancy," George said. "Deirdre is too busy being queen!"

The girls walked down Main Street. Bess stopped at a popcorn cart to buy a bag of caramel corn. She shared some with Nancy and George as they continued on their way.

Nancy tapped the Clue Book with her pencil. "Our main suspect now is Taffy," she said, looking over the suspect list. She had already crossed Shelby and the sea monster off the list of suspects:

1. ~~Crabby Carl's waiters~~
2. Taffy of Taffy's Topiaries
3. ~~Sea monster~~
4. ~~Shelby Metcalf~~

"The woman in Yuks said that Taffy bought a bunch of fake snakes from the store," George said. "That's proof enough for me."

"But we don't know where Taffy is today," Bess said, munching on her popcorn. "How can we question her if we can't find her?"

George pulled an electronic tablet from her small backpack. "Ta-da!" she sang. "My mom let me borrow her mini tablet for the whole day!"

"Now we can look up where Taffy lives," Nancy said excitedly. "Thanks, George."

The Clue Crew sat on the bench while George did a search. She typed Taffy's name, then did her best to spell "topiaries."

Nancy and Bess peered over George's shoulder as Taffy's website appeared. The home page was filled with pictures of lovely green topiaries. It also showed Taffy's address.

"Taffy's gardening studio is only a few blocks away!" George said. "Let's go."

"Wait, George," Nancy said. "There's something else I want to look up."

"What?" George asked.

"Deirdre told us she wrote about her party in her blog," Nancy said. "Maybe she posted some pictures with clues too."

George found Deirdre's blog, *Dishing with Deirdre*. There were pictures of kids having fun at the party. There was even the picture of Deirdre and Queen Marissa.

Nancy studied the picture. The mermaid was smiling from ear to ear. Deirdre's hand was raised in a little wave.

"Why are Deirdre's hands so dirty in that picture?" Nancy pointed out.

"Maybe she was doing cartwheels on the grass before it was taken," Bess said with a shrug. "If I had a party like that, I'd be doing cartwheels too."

"I guess you're right," Nancy said. Still, something about the picture bothered her. Then, Nancy noticed something else.

"Why didn't Deirdre write about Queen Marissa on her blog?" Nancy asked.

George shrugged. "She probably didn't want to explain about the snake in the pool."

"It did ruin Marissa's big show, after all," Bess put in.

Nancy nodded. "That makes sense." She scribbled everything down in the Clue Book.

"Now let's find Taffy!" George declared.

Bess was still eating her popcorn when the girls reached Taffy's gardening studio. The gate was open so the girls walked inside. What they found was a garden filled with leafy green topiaries. There were topiaries of fish, birds—even cartoon characters.

But where was Taffy?

The girls were about to look for Taffy when Bess stopped at a tall hedge wall with an opening in the middle. A pebbly path led inside.

"There's probably a beautiful secret garden in there!" Bess said excitedly.

Before Nancy and George could stop her, Bess darted between the hedges and down the path.

"Bess, wait!" Nancy called. She could see Bess

racing down the walkway. "We'd better go after her, George."

"Yeah," George agreed. "If Taffy finds Bess snooping around, she might flip."

Nancy and George ran down the same path as Bess, but their friend had already disappeared.

"Where did she go?" Nancy wondered out loud.

Nancy and George were surrounded by tall, thick hedges. At the end of the path were two more paths. One led right, the other left.

"It's like walking through a big puzzle," Nancy said as they chose the left path. They were surrounded by hedges—and all the paths led this way and that.

"I think this is called a garden maze," George said. "I saw something about them on TV."

Nancy and George walked down the winding paths calling Bess's name.

"Where are you, Bess?" Nancy called.

"Come out, come out," George called, "wherever you are!"

"I'm over here!" Bess called back. She tossed a popcorn kernel in the air to show exactly where.

"There!" Nancy said, pointing to the flying popcorn. But when they took the nearest path to reach Bess she wasn't there.

"Something tells me Bess is lost." Nancy gulped.

"She's not the only one, Nancy," George said with a frown. "So are we!"

Chapter

9

SNIP, SNIP, HOORAY!

Nancy and George ran up and down the shaded paths calling Bess's name. They were about to call for help when someone tapped Nancy's shoulder. Spinning around, she saw—

"Bess!" Nancy said happily.

"Let's get out of here," Bess said. She waved her hand in the opposite direction. "Follow me."

"How do you know the way out?" George asked.

Bess held up her bag of popcorn and smiled.

"There was a hole in the bottom of my popcorn

bag," Bess explained. "I've been spilling popcorn on the ground by accident!"

"So you left a popcorn trail!" George declared. "Good work, Bess—even though you didn't mean it."

"Shouldn't we pick up the popcorn along the way?" Nancy asked. "We don't want to litter."

"The birds will eat the popcorn," Bess explained. "I just hope they like crunchy caramel corn!"

Nancy, Bess, and George followed the popcorn trail through the maze until they saw sunlight at the end of the path.

"We're out of here!" George declared.

The girls raced toward the opening. As they burst out of the maze, they saw Taffy. The garden designer looked surprised to see Nancy, Bess, and George.

"Uh . . . hi, Taffy," Nancy said.

"We were just checking out your amazing maze," Bess said.

"I can see that!" Taffy said. "I would have preferred you go inside with a grown-up, but I'm glad you didn't get lost."

"Lost? Us? No way!" George scoffed until Nancy gave her an elbow-nudge.

"Do you make mazes too, Taffy?" Bess asked.

"Just this one," Taffy answered. "I've worked on it for years."

Taffy then tilted her head and said, "Weren't you girls at the sweet half-sixteen party yesterday?"

"Yes," Nancy replied.

"So . . . what are you doing here?" Taffy asked.

"Someone put a rubber snake in the Shannons' pool," Bess explained. "We want to find out who did it."

"And you think it's me?" Taffy asked surprised.

"We did find two fake snakes around your topiaries yesterday," Nancy said. "They looked exactly like the snake in the pool!"

"Only two snakes?" Taffy said, tapping her chin thoughtfully. "I could have sworn I put down three."

The Clue Crew stared at Taffy. If this was a confession, it was the easiest one yet!

"So you *did* bring the fake snakes to Deirdre's party?" Nancy asked.

"How come?" George asked.

"Was it to scare Deirdre?" Bess asked.

Taffy laughed as she shook her head.

"I often use fake snakes to keep squirrels and other critters away from my topiaries," Taffy said. "It's a trick lots of gardeners use."

"A trick?" Nancy repeated.

"Most small critters don't like snakes very much," Taffy explained. "They don't know my snakes are fake, so they run away!"

"Queen Marissa didn't know the snakes were fake either," Bess said. "The one in the pool scared the mermaid away from Deirdre's party!"

Taffy shook her head and said, "That may have been my snake, but I never threw it into the pool."

"But you said you were going to surprise Deirdre," Nancy said.

"Not like that!" Taffy insisted. An excited smile spread across her face. "Would you like to see what my surprise *really* is?"

Nancy, Bess, and George traded curious looks. What could it be? They followed Taffy to where her topiaries stood. Taffy pointed to one. It was trimmed to look like a girl wearing a leafy green crown.

"Presenting Deirdre Shannon!" Taffy declared. "Queen of the Sea!"

The girls stared up at the topiary. It was what Deirdre had wanted so badly. It was a topiary of herself!

While Taffy admired her own work, the Clue Crew whispered about the case. Nancy pulled out the Clue Book and pencil and drew a big line through Taffy's name:

1. ~~Crabby Carl's waiters~~
2. ~~Taffy of Taffy's Topiaries~~
3. ~~Sea monster~~
4. ~~Shelby Metcalf~~

"So that was Taffy's surprise," Bess whispered. "Not the snake in the pool."

"But it was Taffy's fake snake," Nancy said quietly. "If Taffy didn't do it, someone else must have wanted Marissa out of there!"

"How could anyone not like Marissa?" Bess asked. "She's Queen of the Mermaids!"

"I don't know," George said. "But someone got their hands on Taffy's snakes!"

Hands? The word gave Nancy an idea!

She turned to Taffy and asked, "Did the Shannons know about your fake snakes?"

"Of course," Taffy answered. "I needed to make sure the fake snakes were okay with them."

Nancy stared at Taffy. Then she examined the Clue Book. She looked at all the clues and suspects. That's when things began to click!

Nancy turned to her friends. "I know who did it," she whispered. "I know who threw the snake into Deirdre's pool!"

Clue Crew—and YOU!

Can you solve the Pool Party Puzzler? Write your answers in the Clue Book below. Or just turn the page to find out!

First, list your suspects:

1.
2.
3.

Next, write down the name of the fake snake slinger:

_____

What clues helped you to solve this mystery? Write them down below.

1.
2.
3.

Chapter

10

MESS UP, FESS UP!

"It was Deirdre!" Nancy announced.

"How do you know that?" Bess asked.

"Because Deirdre knew about Taffy's snakes," Nancy explained. "Plus, she had dirt on her hands in that picture we looked at. And I'm pretty sure it wasn't from cartwheels."

"It was from picking up a snake in the grass," Bess said, her blue eyes wide.

"And Deirdre didn't even act excited about Queen Marissa," Nancy added. "She didn't even write about her in her blog."

"And she seemed really mad when I called Marissa a queen," Bess recalled.

"Because Deirdre always has to be queen of everything!" George groaned.

"It all fits together," Bess said. "But there's only one way to know for sure. Let's find Deirdre and ask her!"

Nancy, Bess, and George made sure to thank Taffy before they left.

"You're welcome," Taffy said. She then pointed to a flock of birds flying into her maze. "I guess birds really like my maze too."

"Or caramel popcorn!" Bess giggled.

The girls left Taffy's studio and headed straight for Deirdre's house.

"No wonder Deirdre didn't want us to work on the case," George said on the way. "She was trying to hide the fact that she was the snake slinger!"

When the Clue Crew reached the Shannons' house they found Deirdre in her backyard. She was busily taking pictures of her birthday presents. Her new electric scooter stood in the middle of them all.

"Hi, Deirdre," Nancy said.

"What are you doing?" George asked.

"My mom wants me to write thank-you cards," Deirdre said, rolling her eyes. "I'm going to write one thank-you on my blog instead—with a picture of all my presents!"

Deirdre held the camera up to take a selfie with her presents in the background. As she flashed a big smile, Nancy asked the big question.

"Deirdre? Did you throw that fake snake in your pool yesterday?"

Deirdre's smile turned into a frown. "Why would I want to ruin my own party?" Deirdre demanded.

"Maybe because you wanted to make sure there wasn't another queen at your party," Nancy said slowly. "So you threw a fake snake in the pool before Marissa could swim."

"Marissa told everyone she'd be swimming," George added. "What better way to scare her away?"

Deirdre stared openmouthed at the Clue Crew.

She then shook her head from side to side.

"That is totally silly," Deirdre insisted. "I never threw Taffy's snake in the pool—"

"We never said it was Taffy's snake," Bess cut in with a smile. "How did you know?"

Deirdre opened her mouth to speak, but nothing came out. Finally she groaned and said, "Why did I ever invite the Clue Crew to my party?"

"Does that mean you did it, Deirdre?" Nancy asked.

"If so, why?" Bess asked.

"Because I didn't want another queen at my party," Deirdre admitted. "I remembered Taffy's snakes and decided to have some fun."

"It wasn't fun for Marissa," Nancy said. "You ruined her show *and* your party."

"My party?" Deirdre gasped. "My party wasn't ruined!"

"But everyone wanted to see Marissa swim," Bess said. "Now we'll never get to."

"You also blamed your friends for what you did," George added. "Not cool."

"So my party wasn't *perfect*?" Deirdre cried.

"It could have been," Nancy said, "if it wasn't for that icky fake snake."

"Phooey," Deirdre muttered under her breath.

"And after you write your thank-you note, Deirdre," Nancy said. "You should write something *else* in your blog."

"Something else?" Deirdre asked, wrinkling her nose. "What?"

"An apology!" Nancy declared.

The Clue Crew left Deirdre alone in her yard. They were happy they had solved the case and just as happy that summer vacation had begun.

"Now that we solved our first case of the summer," George said, "what should we do next?"

"I know!" Nancy said excitedly, carefully placing the Clue Book into her bag. "Let's have our own sweet half-sixteen parties."

"And be queens too?" Bess asked.

"Sure!" Nancy said with a smile. "Queens of mysteries!"

Test your detective skills with even more Clue Book mysteries:

Nancy Drew Clue Book #2: Last Lemonade Standing

"I don't get it," eight-year-old Nancy Drew said. "Doesn't anyone want lemonade?"

Nancy sat with her two best friends behind their lemonade stand. The table holding a pitcher of lemonade and paper cups was set up in the Drews' front yard.

"Maybe it's too hot," Bess Marvin suggested.

"We're selling ice-cold lemonade, Bess," George Fayne groaned. "Not hot cocoa!"

Nancy counted the few quarters and dimes

in a glass jar. She then wrote the total on her favorite writing pad with the ladybug design.

"At the rate we're going," Nancy said with a sigh, "we'll never earn enough money to buy Katy Sloan tickets."

Bess and George sighed too. Katy Sloan was their favorite singer. When they had heard that Katy's next concert would be at the River Heights Amusement Park, they knew they had to go. But Nancy, Bess, and George had already gone to the amusement park twice that summer to ride the rides. Both times their parents had paid for the tickets. So they would have to buy these tickets with their own money.

That's when Nancy had the idea for a lemonade stand. They even taped a picture of Katy to the table to make them work harder! Bess had written the date of the concert right on it.

"We've been selling lemonade for two whole days," Nancy said.

"And I know our lemonade is good enough," Bess insisted. "I got the recipe from my Pixie Scout cookbook!"

"Maybe that's the problem, Bess," George said. "Sometimes good enough isn't enough."

Nancy glanced over her shoulder at her house.

"If only Hannah would give us her top-secret recipe for pink-strawberry lemonade," Nancy said. "It's awesome!"

"Top secret?" Bess said, her blue eyes wide.

"Even from you?" George asked Nancy. "Hannah has been your housekeeper since you were four years old."

"*Three* years old!" Nancy corrected. "And Hannah is more than a housekeeper—she's like a mother to me."

"Then why won't she give you her recipe?" Bess asked.

"I told you, it's top secret!" Nancy said. She flashed a little smile. "Even from detectives like us!"

When Nancy, Bess, and George weren't selling lemonade they were part of a detective club called the Clue Crew. Nancy even had a special Clue Book so she could write down clues and suspects.

"Speaking of detective stuff," George said with a smile. "I joined the Spy Girl Gadget of the Month Club."

"You joined a club without us?" Bess gasped. "But Nancy is your best friend—and I'm your best cousin!"

"Are you *sure* you two are cousins?" Nancy joked.

Bess and George *were* cousins, but totally different.

Bess had blond hair, blue eyes, and a closet full of fashion-forward clothes. George had dark hair and eyes and liked her nickname better than her real name, Georgia. George's closet was full too—with electronic gadgets!

"The Spy Girl Gadget of the Month Club isn't really a club, Bess," George explained. "I just get a new spy gadget in the mail once a month."

George held up a purple pen and said, "The first gadget came yesterday. It's called a Presto Pen."

"What does it do?" Nancy asked.

"I don't know," George admitted. "I think my little brother, Scott, took the instructions—just like he takes everything else that belongs to me—"

"You guys, look!" Bess interrupted.

Nancy turned to see where Bess was pointing. Walking toward their lemonade stand were Andrea Wu, Bobby Wozniak, and Ben Washington from their third-grade class at school.

"Customers!" Nancy said. She smoothed her reddish-blond hair with her hands and whispered, "Everybody, smile!"

The kids approached, each wearing a *READY, SET, COOK!* T-shirt.

"'Ready, set, cook,'" Nancy read out loud. "Isn't that the kids' cooking show on TV?"

"Exactly!" Andrea said proudly. "You're looking at one of the next teams on the show— Team Lollipop!"

"Neat!" Bess said. "What are you going to cook?"

"Our challenge is to put together a picnic basket," Ben explained. "We're making chicken salad on rolls, potato salad, crunchy coleslaw, and pecan bars."

Nancy was surprised to see Bobby on the team. Bobby's nickname was Buggy because he loved bugs!

"You like to cook, Buggy?" Nancy asked.

"Not really," Bobby said. "My mom made me join the cooking show so I'd stop thinking about bugs this summer."

"How about some lemonade?" Bess asked.

"I'd rather have bug juice!" Buggy sighed.

"I'll have a cup, please," Ben said with a smile.

"One cup coming up!" George said. She picked up the pitcher and carefully poured lemonade into a paper cup. Ben drank it in one gulp.

"Not bad," Ben said, smacking his lips. "I taste lemons, sugar, water, and a small dash of vanilla extract."

"You tasted all that?" Nancy exclaimed.

"I can taste anything and name each ingredient!" Ben said proudly. "Superheroes have X-ray vision, but I have X-ray taste buds."

"Wow!" George said. She offered Andrea a cup, but she shook her head.

"No, thanks," Andrea said. "I just had a cup at Lily Ramos's lemonade stand."

Nancy, Bess, and George knew Lily from school. They also knew that Lily's Aunt Maria owned a chain of famous coffee-and-tea cafés called Beans and Bags.

"What's Lily's lemonade like?" Nancy asked.

"Pretty sour," Andrea said, scrunching her nose. "But her lemonade stand rocks!"

The girls traded surprised looks as Team Lollipop walked away.

"What could be so special about Lily's lemonade stand?" Bess wondered.

"There's only one way to find out," Nancy said. "Let's go over to Lily's house and check it out."

Nancy wrote BE RIGHT BACK on her lady-bug pad. After putting the lemonade pitcher in the kitchen fridge, the girls made their way to Lily Ramos's house two blocks away.

Nancy, Bess, and George each had the same rule: They could walk anywhere as long as it wasn't more than five blocks away and as long as they were together. They didn't mind. Being together was more fun anyway!

"Whoa!" George gasped when they reached the Ramoses' front yard.

Mermaid Tales

*Exciting under-the-sea adventures
with Shelly and her mermaid friends!*

Trouble at Trident Academy · Battle of the Best Friends · A Whale of a Tale · Danger in the Deep Blue Sea · The Lost Princess

The Secret Sea Horse · Dream of the Blue Turtle · Treasure in Trident City · A Royal Tea · A Tale of Two Sisters

Candy Fairies

Chocolate Dreams

Rainbow Swirl

Caramel Moon

Cool Mint

Magic Hearts

Gooey Goblins

The Sugar Ball

A Valentine's Surprise

Bubble Gum Rescue

Double Dip

Jelly Bean Jumble

The Chocolate Rose

A Royal Wedding

Marshmallow Mystery

Frozen Treats

The Sugar Cup

Sweet Secrets

Taffy Trouble

Visit candyfairies.com for games, recipes, and more!